BEYOND STONE AND STEEL

A Memorial to the September 11, 2001 Victims

Brian W. Vaszily

Hard Shell Word Factory

© 2001 Brian W. Vaszily
ISBN: 0-7599-0512-6
Trade Paperback
eBook ISBN: 0-7599-0510-X
Published December 2001

Hard Shell Word Factory
PO Box 161
Amherst Jct. WI 54407
books@hardshell.com
www.hardshell.com
Cover art © 2001 Mary Z. Wolf

Tuesday, September 11, 2001

THREE BUILDINGS, four planes, thousands dead. Where were you when you heard the news? Where did you go?

I was in bed, sleeping off a long Monday spent churning out cover letters, writing half a chapter of a novel, and pouting during the spaces in between at what I considered a very cruel year for me so far. In March, I had been downsized out of a job at a dying dotcom; all my stock options, the stuff of so much escapist fantasy, had faded to virtual dust. Since that layoff, I had submitted hundreds of resumes for progressively lower-level jobs than my position at the dotcom, but nothing had panned out. Nothing.

The Friday before, one of only two jobs I had even been allowed to interview for was handed to another candidate. After weeks of trying to impress my would-be peers and managers, after preparing a grueling case scenario as part of the interview process, the hiring manager said she had narrowed it down to me and one other candidate, and it was a very difficult decision, but....

But I wasn't good enough. But the world was against me.

Also in 2001, no less than thirty literary agents had turned down representing the novel I had spent five years writing.

"While your work may not be right for us, we encourage you to keep pursuing an agent, as it may be right for others," came the form letter rejections. "It is a compelling work with strong characters, but..." came the personal rejections from those few who actually read my submission.

But but but. But I was insignificant. But I sucked.

But I could go jump in a lake.

When you are feeling sorry for yourself, all the incidents and occasions that are part of the normal challenges of any life escalate into yet another scheme in the great conspiracy against you.

The severity of my ten-year old son's tics increased – the doctor said it wasn't Tourette's Syndrome, just a few tics that would likely pass after adolescence – and with the worries that provoked for him, I realized it was part of the cosmic plan to level me.

The fuzzy little puppy I had given him as a birthday present in February... "Dogs are fun, but also a big responsibility"… had mutated into a nipping, yapping, gnawing delinquent larger than our house who firmly believed the motions of training were conducted merely for his entertainment. I, designated Chief Trainer, then later Sole Trainer, figured the handsome devil had been sent to further torment me.

The engine warning light in my car had been glaring in my face for two months, and I knew if I paid a shop to estimate the required repairs, their estimate would exceed my available funds by a factor of ten. So I didn't.

Our bills were piling up, earwigs appeared in more and more cracks and crevasses of the house, three of my contact lenses ripped in the space of one week, and… Woe, in other words, was me.

I was in bed. The phone startled me from my gradual awakening, and it was my wife.

"Did you hear what happened?" she said.

I sat up at the urgency of her tone. "Are you okay?"

"Planes hit the World Trade Center in New York! And the Pentagon in Washington!"

For a moment I was relieved. She was in the office of the school where she's a director, and she was okay. My son and my stepdaughter were okay. My mother, grandmother, sister and her family, ex-wife, best friends and everyone I cared about were okay. They weren't there, in New York. They were all here, in the Chicago area. They were all okay.

"They're saying it's terrorists and they might have other planes!" she continued.

Now I cared.

My mother worked in the second tallest skyscraper in Chicago. My brother-in-law worked across the street from the Sears Tower, and my best friend and his wife lived in a high-rise near it.

"The kids–" I started to say.

"I called their schools. They're fine," she responded. "They're keeping them inside. Go turn on the news!"

I had visited the World Trade Center on a business trip. I stayed at the Marriott Hotel right across the street.

There were people in those buildings.

Lots of people. Only then did that dawn on me.

"I'm calling my mom," I told her. "I'll call you back in a few. I love you."

"Love you, too."

I phoned my mom.

"Yeah, hello!" she shouted into the receiver.

"What are you still doing there!" I panicked back.

"They're evacuating us now! I've got to go. I'm fine, talk to you later. Love you."

"Love you, too."

We disconnected.

Images I didn't want to imagine played in my head.

I stumbled to the washroom, forced my contact lenses in, and ran downstairs. Our cable TV had been cancelled in my effort to budget, and our old rabbit-ears antennae only pulled in ABC with any color and clarity. And there was Peter Jennings, and behind him my first image of the catastrophe: the upper floors of one of the World Trade Center Towers engulfed in black and gray smoke, with flames spurting out of an obviously massive hole about three-quarters of the way up. And the twin tower behind it...the twin tower behind it...gone? The thick plume of smoke started on the ground and stretched to the sky–was it concealing the other tower?

"The South Tower has collapsed," Jennings or some reporter seemed to answer me in passing.

And I didn't believe it.

I didn't disbelieve it.

It just made no sense. It was as if they said the sun did not rise that morning. The World Trade Center was monolithic, powerful, eternal. This was the United States of America.

Jennings and team said a different plane struck each of the towers. They said a third struck the Pentagon. Boeing 757s and 767s with passengers on them. They showed the images, but none yet of the second plane hitting the second tower. And like millions of Americans, millions and millions of people worldwide, I listened. I watched.

I thought of my mother, my brother-in-law, my

best friend in downtown Chicago. Nothing bad had happened there. Yet? I thought of my kids and wife out here in the suburbs with me.

What if? What if? What if?

I didn't believe it. I didn't disbelieve it.

I do not recall what Jennings was saying as the smoke suddenly began to billow more violently around the standing North Tower. He was in some train of thought, and he continued speaking on that train for a few seconds as the tower collapsed. Then he recognized that the second tower was collapsing. I had watched it all, but it took Peter announcing that it was falling before I realized I was watching it fall.

Oh.

Oh my God. There are people in there.

Paranoia and pandemonium across the country. In each of our hearts. Another plane – or was it more than one – still unaccounted for, somewhere over the U.S., and most likely hijacked. All airports shut down. The Disney parks, state capitols, Space Needle, St. Louis Arch, and hundreds of other heavily populated American symbols evacuated.

People draining out of downtown Chicago and other metropolises. An explosion at the State Building in D.C.? The President on his way in Air Force One from Florida? Five or ten or twenty thousand dead? Osama bin Laden, Osama bin Laden, Osama bin Laden? The hijacked plane accounted for: United Flight 93 has crashed in a field outside

Pittsburgh, PA.

And images.

Images upon images upon images. A short while after the North Tower collapsed I saw, for my first time, the footage of the second 767, Flight 175, cruising toward and then crashing into the South Tower – the second tower hit but the first to collapse. The nose of the jet seeming to clear through the building and momentarily jutting out the opposite side. And then the expanding ball of flame, frame-by-frame. A series of images captured over the course of seconds that Americans and the world would witness countless times thereafter, from multiple angles, on TV and the Web, in newspapers and magazines, and especially in our heads.

I saw the wide-shots, and later the close-ups, of human beings dangling out the World Trade Center windows, and leaping from them, and falling like sticks, their suit jackets, dresses and hair flapping against the wind.

The gaping hole in our nation's impenetrable military fortress, the Pentagon. The black crater in the ground of a farmer's field in Pennsylvania. The man with the backpack and other horrified New Yorkers attempting to escape the monstrous smoke barreling down the street behind them. The dazed but living ghosts covered by the gray-white soot.

The jagged seven-story skeletal remains of the South Tower. A business memo with its edges charred, found miles away from Manhattan. A Palestinian child in an American football jersey cheering at news of the catastrophe. The rubble.

And then slowly, and still, the facts.

The flight departure times. Time of impact. Total number of people on board. Fuel capacity of the planes. Width of planes to the width of the towers. Seconds it took each tower to fall. Total missing. Total injured. Total dead. Height of the towers. Height of their rubble piles. Cost of the recent renovation to the Pentagon that Flight 77 destroyed. Depth of the Pennsylvania hole. Number of volunteers. Names and ages of the hijackers. Average time it takes to earn a pilot license. Locations of subsequent bomb scares. Location of subsequent injuries to American Muslims. Total square feet of frozen skin donated from a Texas hospital to the injured in New York. Population of Afghanistan. Names, occupations and hometowns of the confirmed dead.

Not for hours but for days, the tragedy is all that existed.

It was the TV, the radio, the newspapers, everyone's conversation and thoughts. We gazed upon the images and gathered the facts. We confessed our rage and sadness. We listened to President Bush, Colin Powell, and other national politicians, New York Mayor Rudolph Giuliani and our own mayors, and to scholars, specialists, witnesses, and religious leaders. We learned about a man named Osama bin Laden and something called the Taliban.

We craved revenge and, simultaneously, peace. We cried for the fallen. We cried for the heroes – fire fighters, police, volunteers, and those passengers who, knowing they were to die, overpowered the hijackers on Flight 93 and averted the death of many others.

We looked to the skies and cringed when the first commercial airliners returned there. We cringed at news of Arab-Americans being harassed or attacked by homeland terrorists. We cringed staring up at any tall building.

We sang our anthems, really listening to the words for the first time in years, or ever. We waved our flag. We lit candles.

We watched the suffering of those seeking the missing, and the suffering of those who loved the confirmed dead.

We heard startling stories of survivors above the hundredth floors and a few survivors beneath the rubble, stories of those who would have been on the deadly flights or inside the towers if it weren't for some quirk of fate. And the tragedy is still very raw, and we continue with all these things.

As the U.S. investigates and retaliates, as the economy wobbles, as security is tightened, and as more people die, new images, facts, declarations and emotions will be added to the story. Bombs are about to fall, and they will fall.

And time will pass. Movies will be made, historians will debate and write books, parents and grandparents will describe the scenes to children. New tragedies will arise. Great feats will be accomplished. And time will pass.

Details of September 11, 2001 will fray, leaving only the most powerful images, new policies and measures of security, and hopefully a lingering spirit of pride and compassion, behind.

But there were people in there, beyond that stone and steel.

I can close my eyes now, as I am sure you can, and see Flight 175 as it is about to slam into the South Tower. We will see this for as long as each of us live.

As I am an American, raised on Hollywood with a heavy dose of Washington, D.C., the temptation will be to replace that picture with fiery images of whatever retaliation the U.S. enacts. An entire city or two of theirs razed and smoldering. Osama bin Laden's head giving way beneath the boot of one victim's father. Revenge, as a screenwriter or a campaign manager would script it.

But there were people in there, and when I set my rage and bloodlust aside, when I stare at the image of that plane, or one of the towers in the minutes and moments before they fell, or rubble where the towers once stood, and really think, I know there is a profound lesson in this.

A lesson beyond locking our national doors tighter and watching the caves of the world more closely. A lesson even beyond feeling grateful for being born into a free country, a prosperous country, the greatest country on earth.

That lesson is that I should recognize all the beauty in my life, all the good people, and all the potential.

I should realize the gift of just being here.

I should cherish being alive.

Those are not routine words for me. My heroes have always been those heavy on drive and determination, who may not have noticed roses exist much less took time to smell them. I have delved into the great texts of various religions, but only as a pseudo-scholar. I cannot read more than a few paragraphs of Deepak Chopra or his touchy-feely kin without wanting to slam dance.

I swear hard at opposing teams during baseball games, earn an average of one-and-a-half speeding tickets per year, have lusted and gambled and drunk a' plenty, and bitch when I'm faced with too many challenges.

I am by no means fit material for a monastery, a pulpit, or even my own self-help tome.

I smoke.

But watching that plane, over and over, I cannot help but ponder what those inside that metal tube were thinking in their final moments. Who they were thinking of.

I cannot help but wonder what victims were doing in the seconds, minutes and hours before the attacks wiped their lives away, and what their actions signify.

I have not been able to escape hearing their voices as if they could speak but once again – not detailing facts fit for CNN, but telling their loved ones what they cherished most in this world, what they hope for the living, what they would have done differently in their lives if they had only known.

If they had only known.

THERE WERE people in there.

Only they can know what their final actions were before the terror and what values those actions suggest. Only they can know what their final thoughts were in the moments before death. Only they can know what was truly important to them. And they are gone. And only those most deeply scarred, the family and friends closest to the actual victims, are qualified to guess at these answers for their murdered loved ones.

But this is a national tragedy, perhaps The National Tragedy. We are all scarred.

Whether tears flowed or we stood somber-faced, we all cried.

We need to imagine these humans as humans, not as an image of an airline jet or several stories of rubble.

And it is not hard to do – they are you. They are me. They are my father, your mother, our siblings and best friends and children. They are us.

I have now been unemployed for over six months. Several more agents have rejected my novel. I have filed bankruptcy. I found a whole colony of earwigs squirming just outside the kitchen door. The dog tore up all of our toilet paper. The economy is in shambles. The Cubs will not win the World Series again this year. And I am a very lucky man.

My son sang an astounding solo in his choir, and just started playing the French horn. My stepdaughter hit a double that scored two runs for her team, and loves to dance. I am married to the most beautiful, patient and caring woman in the world, and she enjoys pool and darts. We are going apple picking this weekend. I have been to Paris. A woman held the door for me today. My mother is one of my best friends. I have a cold beer waiting for me in the refrigerator. This country grants me unemployment checks, and I will find work soon, even if it means serving you double mocha lattes in some cafe. People care about me. I am alive.

They are us.

While I cannot offer details of what really mattered in the lives of the actual victims – even if I had an encyclopedia of facts about each of them I could never know – it could have been any of the rest of us, with any of our details.

The point is, we all share the same essence. Love and longing, for all the different faces they wear, are still love and longing.

I have imagined details of those beyond the stone and steel because I needed to, because no matter where else I've gone and what else I've tried to do since that first footage of Flight 175 heading for the South Tower, my mind keeps taking me inside those planes and buildings. I have full faith that I got their essence right.

Put yourself on that plane.

What and who, on the earth below, really matters to you?

Have you done it?

Have you shown them?

Three buildings, four planes, thousands dead.

They are us, and so suddenly they are gone.

Flight 175, 7:58 a.m.

MAURO RAMIREZ adored his children. When he held his wife on the couch or in bed, she would sometimes whisper her wish in his ear, that he spend less time working and more at home. He would pull her closer and confide that his only dream was for his children to receive a strong education and grow into successful adults.

He has experienced his share of hardship, Mauro would tell her, but all in all it has been a good life. A wonderful life, because he was lucky enough to find her. But, he would add, he wants to make sure his children's lives are even better. Here in the Land of Opportunity, it can happen. It will happen.

Like all parents, Mauro had specific visions of who his children might become.

His daughter, with her quick wit and deep need to always have the last word, a trial attorney standing up for the rights of oppressed individuals everywhere. His son, a professional soccer player kicking the winning goal for the U.S. Olympic team. Okay, he knew these were massive goals, and they were not necessarily goals belonging to his kids (although soccer heroes plastered his son's walls). But a man can fantasize, can't he?

All he really wanted, he would tell his wife after placing the night's kiss on her lips, is for them to be happy. To be happy.

He checked again to make sure his seat buckle was fastened.

Behind Mauro, Janice Wilkington stared out her window at the Logan Airport employee directing their plane with his fluorescent batons. She would someday lead her own company.

That vision inspired her through college, pushed her to hit the library on those nights when it seemed everyone else was primping their hair and painting their faces to hit the local bars. At least it inspired her on most of those nights.

She wasn't sure what her business would specialize in yet – perhaps a market research firm, or perhaps even the chain of pet stores she and her brother, as little kids, used to play that they owned.

If it were pet stores, she'd make sure her dogs and cats came from reputable breeders who treated all their animals humanely. That'd be rule number one, executive edict. She'd even offer her brother a job, but just like when they played, he'd have to report to her. And clean out their cages.

Whatever business Janice eventually opened, she would pour in every ounce of her energy to make it succeed. It wouldn't have to be another Microsoft or Wal-Mart – would be nice, though! – but it would have to be an example to all other businesses in terms of quality of product and service, and how she treated her employees. No wages below double the minimum wage, not even for the most basic jobs. Free daycare benefits, and generous absence of leave policies for both mothers and fathers of new babies. And lots of company outings, since people don't get enough time to enjoy themselves as it is.

A feeling of eagerness welled inside Janice; she'd be completing her studies soon and then starting that first real job, the one paying more – hopefully a lot more – than the internship. She'd pour it on there, and continue pouring it on. Look out world, here comes Janice!

Yes, she'd absolutely lead her own company someday, and it would be a damned good place to work.

"YOU FIXING up your home?" Marla Capinstadt asked the man leafing through a home improvement magazine next to her.

If the economy ever improved and her stock options panned out, she hoped to find a big dilapidated Victorian in some small town that she and her husband could fix up. Paint it pink and blue and white, lay solid oak floors in every room of the house, hang frilly white curtains in the kitchen windows. They'd open it as a bed and breakfast.

"I live in a condo, a high-rise," the man, Bjorn Henson, smiled. "Don't want to have anything to do with maintaining a house, actually. Magazine's just something to look at." Instead, Bjorn dreamed of visiting every major winery in the world. He'd start with France, of course, and work his way across all of Europe. Then he'd hit Napa Valley – he'd been there once, but only briefly – and sip his way across North America. On to South America, whose wines had steadily improved over recent years, then over to Australia and Asia and the most exotic destinations. He had it all planned out.

"Why? You happen to be a carpenter?" Bjorn asked Marla.

She chuckled. "Not yet. I work with computers. But I intend to be."

The Victorian bed and breakfast would have a white spiral staircase on the interior. Whether spiral staircases were Victorian or not. And each bedroom would have a different theme patterned after famous historical figures. A Napoleon Room, Queen Victoria Room, Captain Cook Room, Peter Pan Room. Peter Pan wasn't exactly historical, she knew that, but one of the rooms had to be whimsical. Fun. And she always loved Peter Pan. The dining room, meanwhile, would be pure Frank Lloyd Wright. Not Victorian at all, but it was their bed and breakfast, they could design it however they wanted. And every morning, the smell of pancakes and bacon would waft from the kitchen into that dining room, then curl up the staircase and into each of the bedrooms, luring the guests out. Only problem was, Marla and her husband both hated to cook. They ate out way too much. But maybe the Victorian would change that.

"You going to build your own house, then?" Bjorn continued.

"No. My husband and I are going to buy an old house somewhere and fix it up. Make it a bed and breakfast. Just as soon as we get rich."

"Ah, yes. And I'd love to spend a whole month there, just as soon as I get rich." Bjorn winked at Marla, and she grinned back. They continued talking.

WHEN ERICA Bristle's daddy asked her on her recent fourth birthday what she wanted to be when she grew up, Erica said, "A million-billionaire." When he asked her what she'd do with all that money, Erica said, "I'd buy you and mommy a ship with a pool, a mansion all for Shelty, and every game that ever existed for me. And I'd get grandma a pair of golden slippers." Shelty was their collie.

Erica loved to play board games like Candyman and Chutes and Ladders. In fact, her daddy, warm and tall next to her, had promised to pull out a portable version of Connect Four as soon as the plane was in the air, and she hoped she'd win.

"LET ME help you with that," Dean Flannagan offered Eleanor Borolle as she struggled to fit her bag into the overhead compartment.

She thanked Dean and allowed him to take control of the task while carefully lowering herself into her seat.

The pilot who had greeted her upon entering the plane, with his deep voice, broad smile and shoulders and especially that spicy musk scent, reminded her of her first boyfriend from some sixty-odd years before. He was a quality young man, that old boyfriend – not right for her with his crazy ideas and daredevil ways – but a quality young man nonetheless. Who also kissed like an angel.

She hoped he was still alive, perhaps fishing on a lake somewhere as he so enjoyed doing back when. She made herself hope he had found himself a loving wife who was still with him to this day, and then settled into remembering details of their very first date together.

Dean Flannagan liked his job. Some days he even loved it. On every flight there seemed to be at least one rude person out to ruin his mood, but far more common were the good people that made it all worthwhile.

These passengers – whether destined for business deals, sun and fun, family or friends – deserved his full attention, even on days when it took all of him to give it to them. In fact, even with the airline's cramped seats and bland food opposing him, Dean considered it his mission to make customers comfortable enough to sleep, work, read, or chat.

"Never underestimate the value of helping someone have a better day," he once told a rookie flight attendant. And though he used to dream of being a movie director, helping people have a better day through his Hollywood blockbusters, he was still often surprised with how content his job made him.

However small his acts – a pillow tucked under an old man's snoozing head, a grape lollipop to calm a frantic child (and the passengers around the child), a soothing reassurance for a petrified flyer that all will be fine – he did make a difference. And in what other job would he get to meet so many interesting people? A man who climbed Mt. Everest, the woman who created the Vietnam Memorial in D.C., an old soldier who fought in the trenches during World War I, and even a woman from Poland who made a full-time living off of writing poetry. And who else could say they served bottled water to Bob Dylan, a cold hamburger to Stephen King, two warm Cokes to Chelsea Clinton, and the latest issue of Sports Illustrated to Monica Seles – all within the same week?

Dean stood at the front of the 767 aisle and surveyed the passengers settling into their seats, their conversations, their novels, newspapers and magazines.

A group of passengers like every other group of passengers upon first glance. But a group of individuals, with dreams, goals, fears, loves and versions of life lived absolutely different from any other, upon even the briefest consideration.

Mothers and fathers, grandparents, uncles and nieces and cousins. All of them someone's child. All of them with stories to tell, stories worth hearing, testaments to the great joys and challenges of being alive.

Dean wondered what he'd get to hear today, and from whom. That woman in the blue skirt who carried herself with such dignity, the little boy with both shoes untied, that young man who seemed so shy? Always, at least one of them wanted to share something, some small tale worth laughing about, pondering, or even crying over.

He was not wealthy, the world did not view him as particularly important, but his job was good. He liked it.

Some days, he even loved it.

At 7:58 a.m., United Airlines Flight 175 departed Boston en route to Los Angeles. At 9:03 a.m., Flight 175 crashed into the World Trade's South Tower, killing all 65 people onboard.

Flight 11, 8:43 a.m.

I WAS BOUND for Los Angeles to host a half-day presentation. Last stop on this grueling tour, and then I'd be heading home to you.

Instead, I am sitting here watching these men suddenly praying aloud in their strange language. Their words are forced and frantic. Their eyes leap from us to the ceiling, us to the ceiling, piercing both. I know this cannot be good.

All the other passengers know this cannot be good, for they clutch one another more firmly, cry harder, and pray more frantically to their God. The same God? Still, that flight attendant holds the pilot's bleeding head in her arms and whispers it's going to be okay. That man in suit and tie strokes the hand of a younger man in jeans and a tee shirt and tells him don't worry, he will hold his baby again soon.

Out the window I see Manhattan approaching on

the horizon, and I see our plane is getting low. Too low.

This cannot be good.

They stand there with blood on their knives, threatening to lash at us again with one side of their mouths while the other side beseeches God. Up front their cohorts guide this plane toward some devastation. I feel it.

These will be my killers. Killers praying to God before they kill. What has happened to them that all our tears, our pleas, all this warm and begging flesh cannot move them? And yet they pray?

What God smiles upon killers?

So many have suffered so much, and not become such monsters. My grandmother's cousin who survived the Holocaust. My uncle who survived the prisons of Hanoi.

How does a child grow into such a monster? Not being bathed in enough kisses from mother? No passionate caresses from a first lover? No freshly baked bread, children's laughter, or deep breaths of nature on a sunny day?

A sunny day.

I remember the day of our longest bike ride, when the trail ended at the edge of the country and we veered onto a small and nameless road and just kept going west. To see how far we'd get. We only had fourteen dollars, banana chips and our bottles of water between us, but the day was perfect and we were perfect and we kept peddling.

When I rode behind you I watched you, the way the muscles moved in your legs, the way your hair, always so neatly combed, blew in the wind. The sweet smell of young field corn and blossoming wild flowers became a part of you, as did the blue skies enveloping us and the whir of the birds and invisible beasts that we whizzed by.

When we found that abandoned old barn leaning to the south and you suggested we go inside to investigate, I said no.

I was afraid it would collapse. But you said nothing could go wrong that day and you tickled me and I protested but let you pull me inside. It smelled of damp boxes, lots of damp boxes, but somehow even that was a good smell.

You laid me down in ancient hay and we made love. I made love to you and the beautiful world through you. You made love to me.

I told you the next morning as we walked our bikes back down that country road, too sore to pedal just yet, that I fell asleep immediately after making love, as you had. But I did not. I watched a small gray mouse scurrying across a ledge. Through a crack in the wood the setting sun caused a beam of light, and I watched that beam sweep slowly across the dusty floor; just as it reached your toes the sun disappeared. I watched your naked chest, rising and falling with each of your breaths. And then I fell asleep.

I understand their intention now.

I know why they have stopped threatening us. We are headed straight for Manhattan.

For the towers.

Oh God.

Oh God. Do not let this turn us into them. Erase the monsters, but not the lands they spring from. They spring from all lands. I have nieces and nephews. That man has a newborn baby. They do. We all do.

Everyone understands their intention now.

Some are leaping toward the cockpit doors, some are crying out their good-byes to those they love, some are grasping for the solace of another. A few are sitting here as still as I.

I will remain still, and close my eyes. Let's take that bike ride again, my love. Let's go beyond the barn this time. It is such a beautiful day. Such a beautiful, beautiful day.

At 7:59 a.m., American Airlines Flight 11 departed Boston en route to Los Angeles. At 8:45 a.m., Flight 11 crashed into the World Trade Center's North Tower, killing all 92 people onboard.

Brian W. Vaszily

North Tower, 8:44 a.m.

MELISSA RYAN logged onto her computer, where she scrolled through the customary glut of emails complimenting, criticizing or requesting more information about her firm's services. All in the coming day's work. Then she smiled.

Beaming out of the mass of messages was one whose subject line read, "Ok, I finally got here, now what?"

It was from her mother in Detroit, who Melissa had finally convinced to sign up for Internet access after years of daughter-to-mother lectures on how the Web opens doors to unlimited information, easy and rapid communication, and especially some fantastic shopping – without even needing to fix her hair.

She laughed aloud, recalling her mother pondering, "How do they get all that stuff through a bunch of wires so darned fast?" As a little girl,

Melissa had asked her mother a very similar question: "How do they fit all the people and things through the cords to our TV?" Back then, her mother patted Melissa's head and said, "Some magic called technology." Which is exactly how she answered her mother's question about the Internet thirty-some years later.

She was about to click the message open when an unusual rumble, and a piercing sensation, drew her eyes off the screen and out her office's ninety-fourth floor window.

IN HIS OFFICE two stories above, David Chen took a second sip from coffee finally cool enough to enjoy. He was trying to focus on a memo from the Chief Technology Officer explaining some new procedure, but he couldn't get his mind off that morning's racquetball game against his best friend, Lui.

Every Tuesday morning they played racquetball at a nearby gym; every Tuesday morning Lui whipped his butt. It was Lui's searing backhand that always did him in.

Okay, David admitted to himself with a third sip of his coffee, it was also Lui's prime physical condition while he lugged those extra pounds in his middle around the court. He would no longer gorge on pastrami sandwiches at lunch, he vowed. Today would be the last such sandwich.

Starting tomorrow, he would only eat salads.

Starting tomorrow, he'd also focus hard on improving his backhand.

He turned to face the unusual rumble.

NATASHA SOBYNSKI greeted the man who had just stepped off the elevator with the same receptionist's line she had delivered to thousands of other corporate visitors before.

She knew the tone of her voice was different, however, and she blushed. Because this man, with his wavy brown hair and puppy-dog eyes, was cute. Very cute. He wore no ring. His gray suit fit his tall frame well.

With her short frame and blonde hair, one of their kids would be blonde and the other brunette, and they'd both probably be average in height. But certainly not average in looks. They'd be a gorgeous girl and boy. And smart.

Natasha saw herself and this man walking hand-in-hand in Central Park fifteen years hence, discussing their kids' college education–

"Beautiful morning, isn't it?" the man said, shifting his briefcase from one hand to the other. Beautiful smile, too.

"It's gorgeous," she replied. "Wish we weren't stuck in here."

She kicked the roller of her chair – could her "we" sound any more forward?

"Make a point to get out for lunch today," he

replied, rapping his knuckles on her desk.

Just as Natasha was wondering if there might be an invitation somewhere in his advice, just as she felt her face burning brighter, the rumble.

They simultaneously turned toward the wall it seemed to emanate from.

ELSEWHERE ON those upper floors of One World Trade Center, Enrique Morales flipped through the pages of a college course catalog, determining which computer classes he could squeeze in between his job and the time he insisted on spending with his wife and son.

Seated at a large oak table for a meeting about to commence, Amanda Sorensen made a mental note to call her sister as soon as the meeting concluded. She would apologize for being so crabby the night before, and invite her to dinner on Wednesday.

Becky Goldman stood by a copy machine with Andrea van Zelt, the two of them laughing about the antics of each of their cats.

Becky's tabby thought she was a dog, running to the door and meowing whenever she heard footsteps from outside. Andrea's twin Persians, meanwhile, very much had the mind of cats – they wouldn't eat unless their food dish was placed directly in front of wherever they happened to be lying.

And in a washroom – same time as every other working day, same old stall farthest to the left – Bill

O'Malley sat reading the last lines of a magazine article about improving wide-lens photographic technique.

That was his passion.

Photography, particularly pictures of dilapidated buildings from rural New York and beyond, and someday, though no one but his wife knew this, he intended to publish a collection of his works.

Ahmed Raheef – everyone called him Rah-Rah because he always seemed in the best of moods, even that day a year or so earlier when the entire network crashed – insisted the Yankees would take it all again this year. They had the hitting and pitching, and they had the post-season experience Seattle lacked.

"If that game where Cleveland came from twelve points behind in the ninth inning is any indication," he teased James Fredericks, a consultant from the West Coast and rabid Mariners fan, "Seattle will completely slump when the Yankees turn up the playoff pressure."

James pointed at the newspaper spread open to the baseball standings on his cubicle desk and said, "If that unbelievable record is any indication, Seattle will roll over the Yankees and any other team standing in their path."

"We'll see," Ahmed said.

And then the rumbling.

ELENA KARPOV hung up the phone. Another satisfied customer, until the next time he called.

Opposite the side of the tower where the plane would enter, she gazed out her window upon the Manhattan landscape. Beyond it.

In a classroom in a school too distant to see even from these heights, on this clear day, her nine-year-old daughter was perhaps just settling into her desk after reciting the Pledge of Allegiance.

It was a new desk in a new school year with a new teacher. Her daughter had come home with reasonably good grades the previous year, but this was fourth grade now. Fourth grade, everyone said, was one of the most difficult of all school years, when all the basics learned in prior years must be pulled together to grasp more abstract concepts.

Elena worried.

Just the night before while struggling through homework, her daughter made clear her dislike for math. "Hate it, hate it, hate it," she said. Would she get frustrated enough to give up entirely and fail the class?

Would that failure taint the love she has for her other subjects, and lead to her dropping out of high school if she even reached that point? Would her happy-go-lucky attitude change, and would she lose all her friends, and—?

Elena caught herself. She worried too much. She

had to stop that.

As long as her daughter had her – not to mention a wonderful grandmother and grandfather – everything would be fine. She might struggle through a class here or there, experience rejection here and there, and that would be okay. That would be good, actually, as that's how character is built.

Yes, with her Backstreet Boys folder and glitter lip gloss and her fervor over every pop song on the radio, her daughter, staring at a chalkboard somewhere off in that distance, would grow up to be a strong woman. A veterinarian, a singer, a housewife or a Pizza Hut manager – whatever, as long as she was happy.

Elena picked up the phone to make her second business call of the day, but an unusual rumbling stopped her short. The rumbling became a roar.

For Elena, as for Melissa, David, Natasha, Enrique, Becky, Andrea, Bill, Ahmed, James and all the other human beings who seconds later would be taken from this earth, from family and friends, there would only be the briefest moment of paralysis.

For those who saw the nose of a 757 heading directly toward them, and for those in the plane's incoming path on and around floor 96 who felt the tremble and heard the roar, there would be no time for consideration of impending doom, nor reflection on things unachieved in their lives. Just a brief incomprehension and then whatever world waits beyond this one.

Instead, their last clear thoughts as humans would be another slice of the good lives they tried to lead, as representative of that life as any other slice except that it was, unknown to them, their last.

A brief memory about mom, a memo requiring typing, a bill to be paid, a daughter to be raised.

At 8:45 a.m., One World Trade Center was hit by Flight 11. Thousands in the tower were killed.

Flight 77, 9:42 a.m.

Q. IF YOU, Diane Delray, could say one more thing, what would it be, and to whom?

A. People always said I talked too much, but now, with this, how come it's like I never said anything?

I always meant to tell my cousin it was me who turned him in. For his own good. I know he ended up in prison, but he was going to end up dead. He even asked me once if I have any idea who, and I couldn't bring myself to admit it. He would've understood, eventually. I should have written that letter.

But that's not my one more thing. There's so many "one more things." I wish I had just one of them.

I wish I could have told my kids more about their daddy. Some of the good things.

I never told them the good things. How he once

stood up to three men, all of them nearly twice his size, who were harassing me. How he could make anyone laugh. He had such a sharp wit, he even brought a judge to tears right there in her court. And the man had pipes, too! From Barry White to Sinatra to Robert Plant, the man could sing! Sometimes his voice alone would make everything else okay. Of course, he definitely knew how to use his body, and mine. I wouldn't have told the kids that part. But he was so full of potential. They came from a man who could have done so much. That's something they should have known.

But that's not my one thing, either.

Maybe I would have just told them I love them. Told them just one more time I love them.

Q. IF YOU, Byron McMullin, could change one thing in your life, what would that be?

A. God, there is so much...

I would have changed the way I treated my ex-fiancée. Less yelling, more flowers.

I would have visited my grandmother more often; such a simple thing made her so happy, and the stories she had to tell! I would have changed my career, because I wanted to be a forest ranger since I was a boy.

I would even have changed the tires on my neighbor's car, which I put off doing for over a year now. So, so much.

But if I could only have changed one thing, it would have been my perspective.

I know that sounds so general, maybe too ambitious. But I would have. I intended to.

Of all the stupid things, it was a TV commercial that made me realize that's what I needed to do. A Diet Coke commercial, where this woman and her husband are all dressed up and heading to some fancy party. It's pouring outside, she trips and falls, and her expensive dress and her primped hair are all drenched in mud. She doesn't bitch, she doesn't cry. Instead, she just laughs. Laughs and laughs. And so does he. A Diet Coke commercial! I don't even pay attention to commercials. And I don't drink Diet Coke. It must have caught me on the right day, at the right time. I guess it did.

Earlier at work that day, my computer completely froze up. The IT guys had to shut it down to fix it, and I lost half the data I'd been inputting for hours. I didn't laugh. I cursed the IT guys. I cursed Dell Computer, my boss and everyone around me.

At lunch, the Subway Sandwich girl put vinegar and oil on my turkey sub when I asked her not to, and I cursed her. And then her manager. Some kid cut me off on the drive home and I made a point to catch up to him just to present him with my middle finger.

When I arrived home, the garage door wouldn't open fast enough, nothing but bills and credit card offers in the mail, the garbage in the kitchen stank, and the cats had scratched the woodwork around the washroom door.

I didn't laugh and laugh. I cursed everyone and everything, including my whole rotten life. I grabbed a soda – a Pepsi, actually – and sat down to watch TV. And that Diet Coke commercial appeared.

I vowed to start off by taping bold reminder messages all around me, wherever I went. A message on my car dashboard that said, "Rise above it!" A message on my computer at work that asked, "In the scheme of things, is it really worth the stress?" A message on my bedpost that read, "I'll bet that's not worth losing sleep over." Messages saying "Smile" on my hand if need be.

I'd start making time to read good fiction again, because I remembered how the way they'd delve into characters in even the most tragic stories uplifted me.

I'd sing along to my favorite songs in the car every morning instead of listening to the stock report.

After work, before TV, I'd take a walk around the neighborhood, just to breath fresh air and see the sky, and maybe I'd eventually escalate that to a jog.

Anytime I felt aggravation welling up inside me, I told myself I'd stop, make a pair of glasses out of my thumbs and fingers, and place them on my face, the way they showed me in kindergarten. Look closely now, Byron, is it worth the frustration? Is it something threatening your life, or the life of one you love? Will the world end because of it? No? Then laugh about it, and proceed.

That's what I vowed to do.

I knew it was going to take time, the change in my perspective would happen slowly, but it would happen. If I just stuck to it.

But the next day I was cursing the IT guys again.

Q. IF YOU, Dorothy Collingwood, could try one more thing, what would that be?

A. I would have tried to learn how to swim. Again.

That sounds crazy, with everything there is to try in this world, but when I was twelve, these two older boys who lived in our condominium pushed me into the deep end of the pool. They knew I couldn't swim, they teased me all the time about never wading beyond three feet. They teased me about everything. I was walking by the pool to get a towel, didn't even know they were around, and suddenly one of them shouts, "Sink or swim!" Before I could even turn, they shoved me and I went under.

They say swimming is intuitive to an infant, since we start our life inside our mother's water, but I was no infant; my mind was firmly set that I could never learn it. So flailing my arms and legs wildly, that's what I repeated to myself there under the water: I can't swim! I can't swim! When you're drowning, it's like someone opened a fire-hose and shoved it down into your lungs while someone else is pumping sludge into your brain. You can't think straight, your body convulses. There's this briefest moment of absolute relief, and then you're gone.

I don't know why neither of them jumped in to help me. Instead, they ran and told Mr. Martin, the security guard, and he's the one that ran all the way back and saved me. Apparently, he dove in for me in a full suit and tie. He administered CPR – told me later he had just learned it a week before – and I gagged and sputtered back to life. It was like the screen of an old tube TV when you shut if off, only in reverse. The world came back to me as a single point of light that expanded outward. For a few seconds I had no idea where I was. All I saw was a bearded old face with white hair ringed by sunshine just inches above my face, and while later I would realize his was the face of an angel, my first reaction was that he had raped me. I screamed through my gurgling and kicked and clawed him away. He backed off, smiling with relief, and calmly kept explaining what had happened. When I finally remembered, I looked around – three or four other people had gathered there, but not the boys – and I broke into tears. He had saved my life.

We lived in that condo high-rise for another two years, and in that time I only saw those boys four or five more times. But never again together. I saw them walking down the hall alone or with their mothers. When they noticed me staring at them they always looked away. Never a word about nearly killing me. And until I was in college, I never confessed to anyone they nearly had. According to Mr. Martin, they ran to him shouting, "A girl slipped by the pool and she's drowning!" So that's the story I stuck with. I was looking over my shoulder while walking and just slipped.

Meanwhile, I became good friends with Mr. Martin. At first I felt I had to, but after awhile I just really did. I'd stand by his desk at the entrance to our building, sometimes for over an hour, telling him about my day at school, complaining about how my mom doesn't let me do anything fun, and even confiding who my latest crushes were. He listened, offered me smart advice that never upset me though it sounded just like mom and dad's, and he never even brushed against the issue of saving my life unless I asked him about it. Except for the last day I saw him. He said he was finally retiring, going to chase after the old widows in sunny Florida, and I made a point to see him off on his last shift change.

We hugged. Crying, I whispered, "Thank you."

He kissed the tip of his index finger and tapped it on my cheek. "Those foolish boys didn't mean to hurt you," he said. "Do yourself a favor – get back in the water and learn to swim someday."

That was the last thing he ever said to me.

Through high school, through college, and for all these years, I've heard those words. I've known he was right all along, and I always meant to do it. I always planned on doing it.

I knew what an accomplishment that would be.

Tomorrow, next week, next month, I will get back in the water and learn to swim.

Q. IF YOU, Nicholas Micolai, could make one more thing, what would it be?

A. I would have made dinner. For my wife.

I never did. Oh, I opened cans of soup or tuna on occasion, unzipped those salads in a bag. Hamburger Helper certainly helped me here and there, and I mixed plenty of macaroni and cheese.

But I mean a six-course dinner from scratch. Every ingredient fresh and hand-picked, and not from a supermarket but the small markets, where specialists exist for every item. The bread shop, fruit market, and patisserie. The butcher shop, winery, and creamery. The farmer in his stall proudly displaying his tomatoes. The man in the boat with fish still swimming on his line. A dinner where every bite would melt her strife away, each more completely than the last. Artichoke bruschetta, Swiss chard pie, bluefish chowder, truffle salad with goat cheese, and stroganoff marinated in Cognac. For desert, palacsintas stuffed with rich, creamy chocolate.

Washed down by Opus One, Dom Perignon and Perrier. Consumed so slowly by candlelight and Chopin, where'd I'd lean over with napkin to wipe the crumbs from the edges of her pretty lips, kissing them every time.

The kind of dinner my wife, who has worked so hard for too long, deserves every night. To have done this for her at least once. That would have been making the sweetest love.

And how I loved her. How I do.

Q. IF YOU, Ellen Tierrablanca, could go one more place, where would that be?

A. I wanted to see the ruins in Egypt and Greece, the Great Wall of China, Machu Picchu in Peru. Cruise through the Amazon Jungle, dine on chocolate croissants in Paris cafes, and do absolutely nothing on the sands of the Seychelles Islands. I wanted Mardi Gras in New Orleans and Carnival in Rio de Janeiro. But my one more place would have been Elburn, Illinois.

A dot of a town set in the middle of cornfields, about an hour-and-a-half outside Chicago. I grew up there. Haven't seen the place for over twenty years, when we moved to California for my father's job. I graduated high school and the very next day we were gone. After spending all eighteen years of my life there, we were just gone.

I had a boyfriend, Keith Ramm, and as we were driving away from Elburn, he tried to keep up with us on his three-wheeler motorcycle on the shoulder. He kept blowing kisses at me through our station wagon window and motioning for me to make sure I write, make sure I write.

I bawled the whole way to Los Angeles. I refused to talk to dad up until Colorado. Of course, I wrote Keith that very day, and every day for weeks thereafter. And of course I never heard from him again. He was a drummer in our high school's marching band, and he said he intended to get a scholarship for the UCLA band and enroll there the following spring.

Well, I did keep in touch with a few of my girlfriends from Elburn for a while, and it turns out Keith started dating my younger sister's best friend not three days after I was gone. Took her to the Sunshine Restaurant right out in front of everybody on a Wednesday night. Last I heard, she got pregnant – but not by him – and he was working for Dale Berenson at the hardware store. That was twenty years ago.

So that's where I'd have gone.

I've lived in L.A., Seattle, and even Vancouver for awhile, but that town, a blink on Highway 47, is still me.

I had my first kiss in the basement of Grace Lutheran Church there. Got caught shoplifting

BubbleYum Gum from Perry's Drugstore, and Charlie Mahler, of all cops, is the one that came in for me. I had the biggest crush on him! Tried my first cigarette behind a grain shed just outside town, and haven't been able to quit since. And I lost my virginity – and not to Keith – in the basement of Connor's Funeral Home. Can you believe that?

Those morning donuts at Sunshine's, I've never tasted any as light or fresh. And I can still smell that Elburn air – ground field corn, freshly cut lawn, clover, who knows what else – but I've never been anywhere that smells quite the same.

It's strange, but I even remember the sun shining differently there. Brighter, but somehow more gentle.

I wonder who's still there?

The place has grown I'm sure, probably turned into another suburb of Chicago with McDonald's and Taco Bell and a Wal-Mart. But I wonder if Sunshine and Perry and all those stores are still on the strip. If our old white house is still standing. I wonder if Keith's still around town.

I should have gone back.

Q. IF YOU, Mustafa Saylala, could learn one more thing, what would that be?

A. I would have learned to play the guitar. So I could hear my favorite songs whenever I wanted. So I could write new songs and share them with other people.

I believe there are words in the soul that can only be spoken through music, and my soul had so much to say. But I always told myself I am too busy. Too busy with job, too busy with home. Too busy with driving, sleeping, eating and watching TV. Too busy turning levers, tapping buttons, pulling cards, and pushing pedals. Too busy saying how busy I am. Too busy to learn how to strum.

And now, so much of me that will never be heard. So much never known.

"Mustafa? He was a postman. That's what he was."

Q. IF YOU, Chi Xu, could do one more thing, what would it be?

A. I would have worked on the jigsaw puzzle with my daughter instead of shopping for a new watch. That is all.

Q. And why didn't you?

A. I never knew. I just never knew.

At 8:21 a.m., American Airlines Flight 77 departed Washington, D.C. for Los Angeles. At 9:43 a.m., Flight 77 crashed into the Pentagon, killing all 64 people aboard.

Pentagon, 9:43 a.m.

I WAS A soldier. Age 22. I was in the Pentagon. And I was just killed.

It surprises me that, if I were allowed to come back for just one day, I would not grab my gun to hunt down my killers with my brothers and sisters in arms.

I would call my mom. For more than three weeks, I have not called her. For almost six months, I have not been back to Texas to see her. And now, never again.

I would call and ask her how her left knee is doing. I would ask her how her job at the insurance office is going, and listen to her tell me about some strange claim a rancher filed and what her friend Brenda in underwriting said. I would ask about her garden, the attic, and how the dishwasher is holding up, and about her neighbor, Mrs. Carson's, right knee. I would tell her how much I was looking forward to her special Thanksgiving stuffing and that pumpkin pie.

And I would answer her questions about me. Nope, Ma, not dating anyone seriously right now. Seeing a couple of girls, actually. One of them is a secretary, like you, with freckles and red hair. Cute and polite as can be. The other one's an intern in Congress. A Democrat, but what the heck. Yeah, I know it sounds like Monica Lewinsky, Ma, but she looks nothing like her. She's a tall blonde, actually. No, don't worry, Ma, I won't let her jeopardize my career.

I'd tell her about my newest old Camaro, my trip down to Key West, and what's in a typical day for me. Ma, I told you before, third class is just a military classification, it doesn't mean I don't eat as well as everyone else. I eat fine. Yes, that includes fruit and vegetables. Yes, Mom, they're green vegetables. Alright, I'll tell them to make sure they don't come from a can.

I'd describe at least some of the good movies I've seen lately, and give her details, for once, on where I was headed next. I'd even tell her about the cut on my forearm. Ma, no, come on, I didn't get it shooting up heroin. I don't do heroin. I got it playing ball with the boys here. Going up for the dunk, like only yours truly can do it, but came down on the rim the wrong way. Yes, I stopped playing. Yes, they helped me clean it up. No, it didn't hurt all that much. Yes, I'm sure I don't have – Whoa! Ouch! Oh man, I'm getting muscle spasms! My jaw suddenly 'eels 'ight... I'm just kidding, Ma. Yes, I'm sure I don't have tetanus.

We'd talk for an hour, more if she was in that mood, and at the end I'd do what I haven't done for a long, long time. I'd tell her I love her.

After that, I'd call my grandma and listen to all her bingo stories, and then I'd call my sister and be reminded of why I never wanted kids. And I'd tell them both I loved them, too.

I'd invite Jimmy, a fellow soldier and my best friend, down to the Hut to help me gorge on an extra-large double-cheese pizza smothered with sausage and peppers (see, Ma, green vegetables), then we'd hop in my Camaro and head down to the coast. The long way. The windy way. On the country roads where you sometimes don't pass another car for miles. So I could floor it. Take it past 150 miles per hour, like I always wanted to do. I know that's not the responsible thing, but hell, I'd still be 22. I'd try to be safe about it, at least for Jimmy's sake since that'd be my last day anyway.

Oh, I wouldn't necessarily know I have one more day once the day started? Well, then I'd definitely do it. And when we reached the ocean, I'd strip off all my clothes and dive right in. Swim out as far as I could go and let the waves carry me back at their own pace. Then kick back on the sand with Jimmy and inhale the salt and sun and the pretty women sauntering by. Damned right I'd still be naked!

Before heading home, we'd hunt down the biggest burgers in town. I'm talking those Angus beef patties thicker than the Bible, where the juice oozes out just by making eye contact with it. A side of fat steak fries and a Bud with that, thank you very much. Then I'd let Jimmy drive us back, and if he wanted to try taking it to 160, well, who am I to stop him?

I'd want to play a game or two of ball. Full-court, up to twenty-one, no ticky-tack foul crap. And hell, it's my last day, so I'd get to win. Then a long, hot shower at home, and when I stepped out of the washroom: "Hey, Marissa, what are you doing here?" Marissa's the tall blonde Democratic intern I told mom about, who might jeopardize my career. "Want a backrub, sweetheart?" she would say. And who am I to stop her?

After the hour-plus backrub, I'd take her out to dinner. Whatever she wanted, as long as it was Mexican. Tostadas and enchiladas, fajitas and margaritas. And more margaritas. Then on to a movie. Something funny. Not the occasional ha-ha funny, but "I can't breathe this is so damned funny!" funny. Another *Something About Mary* or *American Pie.*

And speaking of *American Pie,* I'd, of course, end my one more day with Marissa in my bed. Making love to her for hours. Or if Marissa wasn't available, then with Patricia, the cute redhead with freckles. They're both gorgeous and fun. I'd end the night with one of them in my arms, kissing her neck, caressing her stomach, wondering who the woman will be that I spend the rest of my life with.

Maybe I'd also call my mom one more time, just to tell her goodnight.

Now, If I could come back for two days, that's where you get a better story. Give me day one for the bonding and fun, but send me straight to the front line on day two! I've got a country and its principles to defend, and if I have to I'll personally go and –

But I was a soldier. Age 22. I was in the Pentagon. And I was just killed.

At 9:43 a.m., the Pentagon was hit by Flight 77.
190 people inside the building were killed.

South Tower, 9:49 a.m.

I AM TRYING to go up when everyone is pushing to get down.

I know I should turn now and escape down the stairwell with them.

My body knows.

Like all of them, I have everything to live for. Family to take care of, a world to see, and memories to make. I want to sail on the ocean. I want to be a grandpa.

I should turn around and run with all these people. But no. I must continue going up.

This is not just a job.

These people rushing down past me have jobs. They are accountants, secretaries, maintenance workers, attorneys, and they are leaving their jobs behind to escape. They should. But people up there are depending on me or they will die.

I cannot save all of them, I know that, but I can save some of them.

This creaking! The explosions!

Turn around, damn you! This building might not stand!

Don't you want to inhale the scent of your wife's hair again, feel the brush of her fingertips across your neck?

I do.

Oh God, I do. But they are depending on me. I can save at least one of them.

Up there, beyond that door, there are so many injured, burned, overcome with smoke. I can save them. At least one or two. I can.

"Go down! Get out! Fast!"

Is that my voice urging them out as I continue in? This building is going to collapse.

Why don't I follow my own advice?

I have a life to live, too. I want children, a house with a dog. My mother. My wife. I want to sail on the ocean. A small boat, nothing fancy, with a little cabin to sleep in underneath. I'll buy it used, paint it red and green and call it "Noel." That was my first girlfriend's name, my wife won't go for that. I'll call it "The Mistletoe." We'll sail to the Bahamas. We'll dock in the bay of that small island where I proposed to her. I'll kiss her on The Mistletoe and make love to her. We'll have a baby girl.

But I can save at least one.

"Take my arm! Grab hold of my arm!"

I can save her. This woman probably has kids. Get her on your back, come on. She's probably got little ones in school right now who have no idea. They need their mom. This is my job. Come on!

"Go down, people! Let's move, come on!"

We'll make it out of here. At least I saved this woman.

At least I saved this one.

"Let's go!"

No.

Oh God, no!

Oh God.

No.

"I am so sorry."

I am so sorry.

I want to be a grandpa.

I want to sail on the o–

At 9:03 a.m., Two World Trade Center was hit by Flight 175. It collapsed at 9:50 a.m. Thousands in the tower were killed.

Flight 93, 9:59 a.m.

THE WORLD needs heroes.

You knew what they were planning to do. Something had ripped out all of their human wiring and reprogrammed them into fleshy bombs, intelligent insofar as their target but absolutely ignorant to the breathing world around it. It was not difficult to read their program.

But you knew you and everyone around you were going to die, and still you acted, so that others would live.

And that has to be the most difficult thing of all. Because you had love. You had life. Family, friends, and ambitions. None of them very far away.

As long as that plane was airborne, despite what you had heard about the other attacks, despite what you read in your killers' eyes, you must have believed that there was a distant chance – a somehow – that this could end okay.

A glimmer of humanity might fall from a star and lodge in one of the living bombs' eyes. A U.S. Marshall might suddenly appear from the luggage compartment to blow them all away. Some other passengers might stand and fight and conquer and guide the plane to safety, and you and all the good people with you would live happily ever after.

There had to be at least a speck of doubt that the situation was hopeless, and the speck must have been the greatest mountain there ever was.

In only moments, you climbed it. You crossed it. You overpowered the bombs and guided good people somewhere down below to safety, and they will never even know you moved them.

You, and all those faces around you longing only for the embrace of their loves, died, so that others may live.

The world has heroes.

AND YOU, Joanna Brantner, who did not rise from your seat to overpower your killers, your father is in a nursing home suffering Parkinson's disease.

Every other day, with your job and children and housework and the aches in your back, you still visited him there. You always smiled and hugged him upon entering the room, even when his disease scowled at you and insulted you through his mouth on previous visits.

You showed him pictures of your children, and pictures of his family when you were young. You read the newspaper to him. You wiped the spit off his chin and massaged around the bedsores on his back and when he shook in your arms as you hugged him goodbye you struggled to hold your tears till you were alone in your car.

He will miss you.

And you, Chester Havranek, who did not rise from your seat to overpower your killers, you taught high school history for twenty-seven years.

For twenty-seven years you drove to school hopeful that the messages our past can give us for how to guide ourselves into the future would click with at least a few pupils, those who might become leaders, and for twenty-seven years you drove home having been ignored, mocked, criticized and sometimes even threatened by some, and in particularly tough years, most.

In college, you considered being an attorney, a businessman, a politician and a country music star. But you chose teaching.

Then, after one year of teaching, and then five years, and then ten and fifteen, you considered being an attorney, a businessman, a politician or a country music star again.

But, despite the pay, you stuck with teaching. Because, sometimes, a few students' eyes did open wide as they listened or spoke – there was comprehension. Once in a while, a former student returned to thank you for your dedication and to tell you with some joy where they were in life, in part because of you.

And rarely – but it happened – a former tormenting teen whose eyes were opened further down their road would return to apologize for ignoring, mocking, criticizing, or even threatening you. Now they understood. And despite your battles with administration, despite the fact that you were exposed to cafeteria food for twenty-seven years, those students made it all worthwhile. They will miss you.

You, Arif Eshak, who did not rise from your seat to overpower your killers, every time you noticed an accident on the side of the highways you drove so often, you pulled over to assist them.

Sometimes situations were already under control, and sometimes all they asked of you was to place a call or two on your cell phone. But several times you talked them down from their shock while police and paramedics were still on their way. Several times you wiped blood from foreheads and stepped between potential fights.

You never had to pull a victim from flames or the risk of flames, but you told yourself you would have tried if it came down to it. And if it came down to it, you would have.

No matter what your schedule, or how late you

were, or who they were, you always offered your help. They will all miss you.

You, Alvina Jensen, donated ten hours of your week, almost every week since you were seventeen, to saving abused and abandoned racehorses whose competitive days were over, by nurturing them to health and finding them homes.

You tolerated certain people laughing at this passion, or criticizing you because you were not devoting your time to some other cause. Sometimes even the horses kicked and bit you. To it all, you replied, "They are alive, and someone needs to do it."

And you, George Breckel, served the United States in World War II, and though your ship never saw action there in the Indian Ocean, you were ready and willing to die for our freedom, while some of your best friends did.

Janet Steinberger, you gave blood and plasma routinely.

Adelaide Trujillo, you looked a feared drug-dealer in the eye and told him to keep away from your children and your neighborhood, and when he sneered "Or else?" you said, "Or else me and the other parents here will do whatever it takes to get rid of you."

Lucia Barron, you wrapped and delivered the leftover food from your family's restaurant to a shelter every night.

You, Dominick Gianopulos, coached peewee

basketball and soccer for nine years, without pay, even after your two daughters had grown beyond the teams.

You, Casimir Letts, let your neighbors – a family of five who moved here from Nairobi just months before – live in your house for three weeks when a fire burnt theirs.

With a substantial portion of all the interest on your wealth, Linda Gnadt, you set up a fund for young sculptors.

And despite the fact that you were dirt poor, Michael Storry, you recently gave a hundred bucks to an organization helping battered women.

None of you rose from your seats to overpower your killers, and we all understand.

The world has heroes.

And we will miss you all.

THE WORLD needs heroes.

At 8:01 a.m., United Airlines Flight 93 departed Newark for San Francisco. At 10:00 a.m., it crashed into a field in Shanksville, Pennsylvania, about 80 miles from Pittsburgh, killing all 45 people onboard.

South and North Tower, 8:45 a.m.–10:29 a.m.

AS THEY shoved their way toward the windows their thoughts were hardly thoughts at all. With the smoke and flames and grate of metal their instincts had taken over, pushing them to open and fresher air, to what seemed to their bodies like the only means of escape.

If they had lived, most would describe the moments in which they ran to the windows as black or blank, a mass of commands in the brain too concentrated and rapid to be remembered. Not about love or pain but pure survival.

But as they leaned out the windows, some solo, some sharing their space with others, there came a brief clarity. Fresher air. Blue skies. A world above, beyond, below. They were going to die.

If they remained, they were going to be killed, and if they jumped, they were going to die.

So that was it. Jump.

And after words directed at gods, devils and mortals, their final thought, the very last before each of them leapt, was a wish.

And the wish was good.

Al Torentino wished that his mother, a widow for over a decade, would find a kind man for whom to cook her famous ravioli for the rest of the days of her life. In his mind he saw her face, sweat on the brow, white hair at her temples, but such a proud smile as she placed a dish of that ravioli down before him. The doughy pockets overstuffed with meat and cheese suspended in thick red sauce; she was an artist, like him.

He closed his eyes and caught the tangy scent; he kept his eyes closed to hold that scent, and he jumped.

Dong Li wished that her death would not deter her son from acting. She had been hard on him, insisting he choose a practical major in college like engineering or business.

They had argued just the previous night; he slammed the door on her, and that was to be the last she ever saw him.

"I only want my baby to be okay," she now confessed into the screaming wind.

He wanted to major in theater. He wanted Broadway.

"I know you will dazzle them all," she said,

aiming her words at a scrap of office paper fluttering by, hoping it would carry through the skies and land atop her son's heart.

She jumped.

Marcel Farrenon laughed. A staccato of amusement choked out through metallic smoke, at one-thousand feet on the edge of a ravaged and trembling building, amidst screams and tears including his own.

He and his best friend had jumped from a plane just two weeks prior. With parachutes, of course.

After years of talking about it, they finally gathered the money and courage and did it. His best friend said he'd do the jump again, anytime, hell yes, but Marcel said, "Mission accomplished, but I think that's it for me."

A vision of the parachute not opening next time. And now this.

"Don't ever let fear stop you," was his wish, and not just for his best friend, and he jumped.

Through the pain of her burns and her stinging eyes, Tanya Jordan found her pink rosebush.

It had grown so tall and lush with sweet blooms that Mrs. Halpert, who lived clear across the street, said it was like breathing in heaven every morning.

Tanya wished that Mrs. Halpert and the other neighbors she was blessed with would pamper that rose tree as she had, and whenever the petals and their fragrance opened they would remember the best of her. The peanut butter sandwiches she made for their children, the ear she was always willing to lend. She jumped.

Erica Hoic, ever about the big picture, wished for peace on earth.

Mars Aufmuth wished only for a healthy baby to his pregnant wife.

Jennifer Maisel, referring to her life insurance, said aloud to her husband, some thirty miles in the distance, "Please buy yourself the Harley you've always dreamed of."

Katya Stanislau wished for her father to come to America, still.

Iain Hugh, for the pain to end.

Barbara Pinkerton, for Heaven to be real.

Sandor Svoboda, for his music to be published.

Vince Larro, to again see his daughter, taken too young from this world.

Braxton Smith, for his grandmother to reach one hundred.

Annabel Caruso, to tell her brother she always loved him.

They jumped.

Barry Amenshan, just married one month prior, wished his new bride the house they dreamed of together.

He wished her two beautiful children, a bright purple lilac bush in the front yard, and a willow tree reaching over a creek in back. He also wished his bride a new husband, who would love her as completely as he did. He jumped.

Their burns, the glass in their bodies, their suffering behind them, their feet now moving toward death, their wishes were for children, spouses, lovers, parents, friends, family. For this world, and the next world.

Wishes spoken or thought outright, or an image, a phrase, a scent imbued with wish. And the wishes were good.

They jumped.

And we watched their bodies fall, and their bodies taken, but nothing can take a wish.

The wishes are with us.

One World Trade Center, hit by Flight 11 at 8:45 a.m., collapsed at 10:29 a.m. Two World Trade Center, hit by Flight 175 at 9:03 a.m., collapsed at 9:50 a.m. Between three and five thousand people in the two towers were killed.

South Tower, 11:59 p.m.

I KNOW good people are trying hard above me.

I know how much good people across the world are hoping for me. But it has been hours – or days? – trapped here, and I know I will not make it.

I have choked out this dust, screamed for the pain of this steel and stone crushing my legs. But now my head is all I feel.

The grit coating my forehead, and what feels like a mere scrape by my left ear though I know, because my head is soaked and I smell the blood, it is worse. I no longer feel the rest of my body. It is beyond numb.

My hand goes to my cheek when I command it to, but the skin of my fingers is rough and foreign. My hand has become an object. I am already leaving my body. And it is so dark. An impenetrable darkness.

Perhaps I am already dead.

But I can hear myself shout: "Down here! Help!"

The words stay close to me. I am in a tight space here. I can hear my own breathing, and churning in my stomach. And I know good people are trying hard above me because, occasionally, I hear something from on high. A distant thump or clank.

That's why I shout.

I am alive.

But I will shout no more.

I am dying, already buried, and this is my coffin.

Something exploded in the other tower. It might have been an airplane. Someone said they heard it was.

Jesus.

And so I started to go down. I was on the stairwell, already near floor thirty, but the public announcement said not to worry. They said it was safe to return to our offices.

What am I that I simply obey a voice on an intercom?

I cannot even recall my instincts as I returned to the office. I have been too obedient to invisible voices my whole life, that I know. Too late.

So I returned to my desk, and just as I sat down to call you, the building exploded. The impact threw me against the desk, but I swear in the quarter-second between the explosion and hitting that desk, I had time to think that my butt hitting my chair had somehow set a bomb off.

I suspect no one found me there because I was

hidden behind three cubicle walls, and who was in the mood to search the place before escaping?

I'm not sure how long I blacked out, but when I came to, the office seemed abandoned. Monitors, paper, staplers, pictures, and even insulation boards from the ceiling littered the floors.

Strange that, for a few moments, it all just amused me. Then Ashwani Kapoor from Finance stumbled out of nowhere, cupping his hand over his eye, with blood pouring out between his fingers. He must have been propelled into something sharp. I called his name, but he didn't stop or turn. I don't know where he went, and I never saw him again.

I inspected my own body. A lump the size of a plum on the back of my head, but nothing more. I started to wind my way out of the office toward the stairwell, but near the exit I saw Angel Martizos standing in the doorway of his office with his back turned to me. Just staring out his window. Absolutely still.

Shock.

"Let's go!" I tried to tug his arm.

He's a very large man, you'll remember from the summer picnic, and he wouldn't budge.

"We have to get out of here!" I tried again.

"I should call my dad," he whispered.

I peered over his shoulder, following his gaze out the window.

The blackest storm had swallowed the building,

with pellets of falling flame and hunks of concrete as the rain, and scorched paper dancing in all directions like snow.

Witnessing that smoke I realized its caustic odor was fast increasing; part burnt gas, part drywall dust, part electric fire and other parts I can't identify, I had never smelled anything like that before. It smelled of pure poison.

"You need to get the hell out of here, Angel!" I shouted at his face for the third time.

My stomach churned, yelling at him like that. Not because he's huge, but because he's my manager's manager. Isn't that ridiculous?

"We need to go right now," I tried more calmly.

He lifted his finger and pointed out the window.

"I saw a man falling." He spoke slowly, each word its own sentence. "I could see his face."

I looked out the window at the boiling darkness again. There were slits in the smoke to the blue skies beyond, as if someone were trying to slash their way out.

I did not understand what he had said. A man falling? His face?

The building trembled. Then I understood what he meant.

"We need to get the hell out of here!" I slammed my open palms into his back. The impact pushed him forward a single step.

He turned and looked at me with some

recognition now.

"We're going to die if we don't go now!" I said to his eyes.

He followed me out.

The stairwell was crowded but people were moving steadily. They weren't shoving, as I always imagined they would in an emergency like this.

Actually, through the doors on every floor, two or three people were invited to cut into our section of the line; those who didn't get into our section generally seemed patient to wait at their exit door for the next opening.

Polite drivers at last. And except for some coughing and a man encouraging everyone to "Move, move," they were remarkably quiet.

Most of the people clomping down the stairs around me were stained with sooty sweat. Tenants of the higher floors. Half of one woman's face was burned bright red, her right eye swollen shut, but she kept calm and silent with the rest of us.

I measured our progress down, and my increasing safety, not by floors as much as the distance we were putting between ourselves and the roar of the fire above (I'm guessing the explosion – the bomb or plane or whatever hellish device that was – went off about ten or so stories above our offices.)

Only now, lying here, do I also remember that the closer to the earth we got the more people were starting to cry aloud, and to throw out one-line testimonies and theories about what was happening.

"People are jumping!"

"New York is under attack!"

"This building might collapse!"

I remember that last one clearly.

It came from a woman with blonde hair and a chocolate brown business suit. She had an accent, maybe German or Dutch. She was the one who started pushing.

Can you believe I doubted her? I figured this is the World Trade Center, if a bomb in the basement a few years back couldn't bring it down, a bomb or a plane or whatever it was that struck high up surely wouldn't. It wasn't nuclear, or I'd already be dead.

I felt lucky. Safe.

I was already crying for Ashwani Kapoor, who might have been blinded, and for those I didn't know above us who surely died.

I was already crying at the prospect of soon holding you and the kids in my arms for hours, and being able to live, and doing all the things I always put off doing. To take ballroom dancing lessons with you. To raft down the Snake River with my son. To write a memoir about my dad.

That's when the building started to moan. I think it had been groaning softly prior to that – my senses were more attuned to the smoke and fire – but it let out a sudden and immense metallic creak that faded only to be followed by another and another.

"It's going to collapse!" More and more people started to scream.

Now people began to stumble on stairs and against the walls, though still no one fell because others caught them and took a moment to set them aright.

"Get out, go!" two men shouted as they barreled into us, around us. Police officers going up.

This restored my confidence, only to be obliterated seconds later by an even more grating moan. I felt the building sway.

Behind me, Angel had somehow managed to dial his cell phone as he moved; he cupped it like a microphone, leaving a final message: "…don't know if we're going to make it out. Papa, tell Ma I love her, tell Maria…"

I meant to borrow his phone when he was done. For the first time on that journey down I realized I might die.

I watched you, the children, and my mother at my funeral, with Pachelbel's "Canon in D" resonating in the background.

Remember how we meant to play it at our wedding but we lost the CD? How that piece moves you. Please play it at my funeral. And release the ashes of my body, or burn my favorite books and release those ashes if they cannot find my body, over the Grand Canyon. Take a trip there with the kids when you are ready, and let the spirit of the place fill you as it did to me when I was only sixteen.

We should have all gone there together. Take the kids on the mule ride all the way to the bottom, just for fun.

I started to shove with the rest of them, and I caused a woman to fall. I tried to swing around her; her feet became entangled in mine, and she tumbled between everyone and down three or four stairs. She landed flat on her side and people just kicked past her in their panic to escape. I stepped over her and kept moving.

She was a small Asian woman, perhaps Vietnamese, wearing a long black skirt, black suede pumps and a necklace with a red stone pendant. A garnet or ruby. She howled in her language as feet slammed into her breasts and gut. I saw the fear in her eyes. She couldn't get up.

I rounded the corner, lost sight of her, and then stopped and turned. I crossed my arms over my chest to fend off the swarm.

Angel tried to grab for me, shouting what I had shouted at him earlier: "We need to get the hell out now!"

But I had caused her fall. If I had not, I don't know if I would have returned to help her. But I had.

I forced my way back up to her. She was curled up in a ball now, but a black man, in what might have been a FedEx uniform, was standing over her, trying not to give up on shielding her from the onrush of people.

"Give me a hand here!" he commanded when he recognized my intention.

I bent down, swiping at kneecaps to keep the crowding people's legs away, and we somehow lifted her to her feet. Her face was battered and she couldn't stand straight, but the tide of bodies immediately began to carry her down and away. She turned back toward us and mouthed "Thank you," and through swollen lips I knew she was smiling.

The collapse began as a metal moan and a trembling that, unlike previous creaking and shaking, only escalated in pitch and intensity.

Everyone stopped.

Suddenly, the ground seemed to bounce and then ten thousand freight trains were descending upon us.

I saw mouths crane toward the ceiling in screams but I couldn't hear them. I saw people fall to their knees, their hands clasped white in prayer. Two men clenched one another. Others just stood there closing their eyes to go out in a better place.

The last thing I remember is stumbling through an opened door, out of the stairwell, and landing face-first onto a burgundy carpet. The new carpet smell. My son as a baby, determined to crawl to me on the bedroom floor. And no more.

I opened my eyes here hours or days ago and saw nothing. Pure darkness.

It is like you imagine it – I did not know where I

was or even if I was. Then the first pulse of pain from my crushed legs reached my head, and I was reminded.

I was in Two World Trade Center, and it had collapsed.

I was buried, and could only feel stone and steel around me. Like I already said, I screamed at the pain, at God, at those above this darkness, and I choked. I called out for Angel, for anyone, but no response.

And now I will be silent.

I no longer even feel the top or back of my head, just my face. Somehow that is appropriate. I can feel where you last kissed me.

Is it a miracle I survived whatever happened up there, when I will die alone here anyway? I do not know.

But I can still think, and while I know you can't hear these thoughts, perhaps somehow you will feel them. That is my hope.

Perhaps one of these chunks of concrete that surround my body will find your hands, and you will feel these thoughts through it.

I don't know what I mean.

It is a miracle that I can think at all.

It is a miracle that I have lived.

Please tell my mother she raised a good man. A man who made mistakes, but a man who so desired to improve the world before he left it.

I did not intend to be in sales my whole life, or even more than a few years. I was just trying to give you and the kids some comfort and security. You know that. But it seems so petty now. All those papers and the office equipment scattered across the floor after the explosion seem so damned insignificant.

Why did I let a job I feel nothing for consume so many hours, suck up all my energy?

I could have been writing a book about my father. The world would have one more example of a real hero. It needs those heroes.

I could have spent more time with the kids. Constructing puzzles, pitching baseballs, having silly music concerts.

Remember when the four of us jammed on toy instruments for more than an hour, and how the neighbor's dog barked? You were so smooth on that plastic slide horn, baby. The kids, of course, ignored my rhythm on the tambourine, each inventing their own. That was so much more important than finishing a presentation, making a few more calls, landing any new account.

I see that now.

Please tell my mother I always meant to fix the gutters on her house. I think all they need is a good cleaning and a few nails here and there. It would have taken me only half a day. Maybe you can ask Neil if he'll do it.

Tell my mother I may not have always been the best audience to her advice, but deep down I was so appreciative she was there to give it. How often she was right about things, too. How humbling that I had been educated on so many books, that professors and peers always lauded my brilliance, but she, with a few unassuming words delivered only in love, always made my knowledge seem pale by comparison.

Please let her know.

And remind her, and remind my sister, about the stories I shared with you of my childhood. Building living room fortresses made of blankets and pillows on Saturday mornings – just like our children do – while she cooked pancakes and bacon in the kitchen. Our tubing trip down the river in the Ozarks. The time some neighborhood bullies destroyed our clubhouse in the backyard, but we rebuilt.

I wish I could tell you more of these stories. How I adored this hideous brown, green and red knit hat, but lost it in a department store while shopping with my mom. How I cried, and how she had half the store's employees hunting it down. We never found it.

She told me it had gone to hat heaven, and let me pick out a new and equally hideous winter cap. With bills and work and plans to make it never seemed like these stories mattered. But how they do.

Tell my sister I wish we could have gone out for coffee together, just the two of us, to laugh at our memories. To recall the best of our father, the best and worst of all the weekend trips we took together as kids. Trying to outdo one another's goofy faces in the back seat of the car. Yanking a single strand of mom's hair and then looking the other way. And all those stray dogs we secretly boarded in the garage, in hopes of a substantial reward, in higher hopes of getting to keep them. I think we made a total of ten bucks for all our efforts. And our summers spent on grandma and grandpa's farm.

I can go there now. The morning sun through grandma's gently billowing lace curtains striking my face, awakening me. My sister in the twin bed across from me, still asleep. Absolutely needing to creep over to her, to stick my nose a half-inch from hers and bellow, "Rise and shine!" The loving hate only a sibling can feel. The delightful pain of my hair yanked in her crabby vengeance. And then racing downstairs together, eager to tattle on one another, but all intentions quickly extinguished by the enchanting smell of grandma's baking bread. By the stern expression on grandpa's face.

"You two ready to work?" he'd demand, and our shoulders collapsed. We'd always believe him. Because he always worked – at the butcher shop in a nearby town for eight hours of the day, and then in his fields or barns until night fell, or *Quincy* or a John Wayne movie came on the TV.

But our days there were much more play than

work. After a breakfast always highlighted by grandma's homemade bread topped with too much butter and honey, we'd run outside to feed and chase the chickens. To pet the cows and fail at milking them because we feared their massive legs. To climb trees, invent games in the cornfields, explore further down the creek, leap from the haystacks, and bury ourselves in the field corn crib. That was our Paradise.

Tell my sister I loved her.

She's a wonderful mother, a wonderful person. Tell her.

And our kids…our kids. How can I do this?

I don't want to die.

I don't want to die!

I need to be there for my son! I want to be a father for my stepdaughter!

Why am I trapped down here all alone? Who did this to me?

Where is God?

Tell our politicians to stop at nothing to find whatever bastards murdered me! What did I do to them?

Tell our police to make the devils suffer for this, to crush them all!

I want to live, my love. I need to be there for my son.

I want to be a father for my stepdaughter.

I want to hold you again.

Tell our armies to crush their families and their children so they feel this pain, too! Kill them all!

But no.

No.

I can no longer feel my face. My body is gone. I am dying, my love.

Tell the world to stop the killing. Revenge is a serpent biting at its own tail. Revenge can be justified till the only two brothers left standing on this planet lash out at one another.

Tell them.

Remember how our children laughed at our wedding?

Your daughter, who became our daughter, looked as beautiful as you in her pink dress. She carried herself with such assurance and grace. A little Princess who finally let loose on the dance floor, becoming a nine-year old again, when they played "Mambo #5."

Her joy at the simplest things is divine. The thrill in her eyes when we sat down to a game of Yahtzee. The gorgeous smile on her face when I picked her up from school. That is the purest form of wisdom; she gets that from you.

With that, and her amazing determination, I know she will grow into a strong woman. Strong and happy, successful at what matters to her. I wish I could see it.

I hope somehow I can.

And my son, who became our son, do you recall

the toast he gave us? A ten-year old, standing up on his chair on his own volition, and telling a roomful of adults how happy he is that you are now his stepmother, and wishing us a lifetime of happiness together.

Of course I cried.

I always knew the brilliance of his mind, with his profound questions, his craving for books and museums, his creations on paper, on the computer, and with Lego's. But he demonstrated the brilliance of his soul there. That is more his mother than me.

Tell her that, though I know we were not meant to be together as husband and wife – we were far too young, we did not know what else to do – I always loved her. And I am sorry. She is a beautiful soul, like our son.

He is still blessed with the both of you.

I am the unlucky one.

I am the one lying here unable to move in this cavern of death whose walls I cannot even see.

I don't think I can hear anymore.

I try to speak, I feel the vibrations, but I don't hear my words. I don't hear the crumbling ruins around me, or thumps from the people trying high above. I can't even hear my own breathing.

But still I can think.

Why will I never hear my son sing with his choir again?

Why will I never again take him camping and

invent stories of tree monsters and mud men as he leans against me by the bonfire? Why will I never teach him to drive, play basketball with him when he's better than me, meet his first loves, hear his theories on life as a college student, or share a beer with him?

Why will I never hold his baby, or hers?

Why can't I ever host a ticklefest with them, and you, anymore?

Why can't you hold me?

I am fading in and out, my love.

Like being on the verge of sleep, wavering at the edge of reality and seemingly irrational images.

We were just poolside in Jamaica, ordering jerk chicken from the grill, only my friend Mike was the cook and he couldn't understand me.

I always tried to fall asleep after you in bed, because you'd make me laugh. You always talked so much when you faded into sleep; mostly you were back at your daycare job in those immediate dreams, asking your peers to find a certain file, telling a child not to be naughty.

Sometimes I would whisper things in your ear, to see if they'd enter your dreams. I asked you once if you saw that naked old man, over there on the pier, doing a handstand. From your sleep you said "Oh my God, yes!" and you started to laugh, and of course I laughed.

I hope this wasn't mean of me. I only tried to

make them funny sights, or beautiful ones.

Did I ever tell you how much I loved cuddling you, too?

I know I often protested when you wanted to spoon into me while we watched *Who Wants to Be a Millionaire?* or those Travel Channel programs, but I was only teasing because I saw your desire. I always readjusted myself on the couch. I always wrapped my arm and leg over you and pulled you in close. I felt so whole then.

There is so much. So much, my love.

Do you remember making love between those sand dunes on that small island off Corpus Christi? That sand clung so hard to our scalps and skin, even the ocean refused to wash it away.

"Let everyone know then," you smiled. "Who cares?" And how you'd pout when I beat you at mini-golf or ring-toss, or I'd make excuses when you beat me at Horse or Sugar Spin. No one else knows the game of Sugar Spin, do they? That's our own creation, and yes, you will always be the champ.

So much comes back to me now.

Wandering off the trails with you at Elephant Rock State Park and scaring ourselves with imaginary snakes in the brush. Tossing short glittery skirts and ridiculously patterned blouses into your fitting room at the stores just so I could see you in them. Performing my own special hoedown dance to the tune of "Cotton Eyed Joe" at your request. The silly smirk you wear as you're brushing your hair. Water fights in the washroom. Lewd poses on a great sculpture. Water falls from ceiling fans. Broken down cars. Candlelight backrubs. Invented words. Plastic carrots. Fishing. Dancing. Walking. Painting. Skiing. Stroking. Driving. Kissing.

So much more I wanted to do with you.

Life we should have shared.

I hope you find love again. I hope you always see the beauty in this world, and share it with our children, with all those you love, and with all the strangers.

I intended to take you to a bed and breakfast this December. A farmhouse with deep woods in back and miles of field out front.

I stayed there once, alone, when we broke up for those few months. I tried to work on writing a book there, and another woman staying there alone tried to work on me. But nothing happened. Nothing at all happened. All I could think about was you.

How I wished, when I took those long walks through the whispering oaks and maples, that my solitary arms were filled with you. How I wished, as I tried to ignore you by reading magazines, that you were in that empty chair across from me. How I wished that we could sit together on a porch like that, on a metal bench like that, and inhale such sweet air together when we got old.

Up until today, I thought those wishes would

come true.

I was going to buy you a rose and a small card, in which I would only write the dates of the surprise weekend inside of a heart. I was going to place the card and the rose on your pillow, so you would see it when you got home from work. And when I got home, I would drop hints here and there, but I wasn't going to tell you where we were going till we finally got there.

If somehow you can hear me, tell that to the world. If nothing else, that they should know.

The reservations were already made.

~*~

Brian W. Vaszily

IN FOURTH grade, Brian Vaszily's first story received an award in an Illinois contest where the poet Gwendolyn Brooks told him, "You've really got a knack for this, young man, keep working at it." He has kept working at it, with fiction and non-fiction contributions to various magazines, newspapers, and a book anthology, as well as two unpublished novels. He has also been a stock boy, deli clerk, cashier, professional carrot juicer, coffee telemarketer, Navy recruit (medical discharge), bookstore associate, waiter-in-training, technical writer, copywriter, communications manager, Internet strategist and project manager, to name a few.

In early 2001, he was downsized out of a struggling dotcom company, and despite sending out hundreds of resumes, has been unemployed through November 2001. "I am convinced now that being kept out of work is part of some greater plan allowing me the time and energy for *Beyond Stone and Steel,*" he states. "My wife and I have been challenged with finances and all, but, as September 11 has made me aware, that's not important. Not compared to having family and friends who love and support you, or to pursuing your passions. Not compared to being alive. I am very lucky. And if this book makes just one reader realize what a precious gift life is, if funds from the book bring a smile to even one child of a victim, I will be luckier, and happier, still."

Brian grew up in Chicago, earned his B.A. in English from Northern Illinois University, and currently resides in a northwest suburb of Chicago, where he absolutely adores his wife, son, stepdaughter, two cats, and even his un-trainable dog. *Beyond Stone and Steel: A Memorial to the September 11, 2001 Victims* is his first published book.

Write the author at Brian W. Vaszily, PO Box 958742, Hoffman Estates, IL 60195-8742